Franken (Illustrated) for kids

—

Mary Shelley

—

Adapted for kids aged 9-11 Grades 4-7, Key Stages 2 and 3 by Lazlo Ferran

Classics adapted by Lazlo Ferran:

The Mysterious Affair at Styles – Adapted For Kids
The Mysterious Affair at Styles – Adapted For Kids – Large Print
The Mysterious Affair at Styles – Kids Colouring Book
The Mysterious Affair at Styles – Kids Fun Exercise Book
The Mysterious Affair at Styles – For EFL/ESL Level B2 Students
The Mysterious Affair at Styles – Vocabulary Stretcher
The Secret Adversary – Adapted For Kids (US and UK Editions)
The Secret Adversary – For Kids (US and UK Editions) – Large Print
The Secret Adversary – Kids Colouring Book
The Secret Adversary – Kids Fun Exercise Book
The Secret Adversary – For EFL/ESL Level B2 Students (US and UK Editions)
The Secret Adversary – Vocabulary Stretcher (US and UK Editions)
Frankenstein – Adapted For Kids
Frankenstein – Adapted For Kids – Large Print
Frankenstein – Kids Colouring Book
Frankenstein – Kids Fun Exercise Book
Frankenstein – For EFL/ESL Level B2 Students
Frankenstein – Vocabulary Stretcher
MacBeth – Adapted For Kids
MacBeth – Kids Colouring Book
MacBeth – Kids Fun Exercise Book
MacBeth – Adapted For Kids – Large Print
MacBeth – For EFL/ESL Level B2 Students
MacBeth – Vocabulary Stretcher

Other books by Lazlo Ferran:

Ordo Lupus and the Temple Gate
Too Bright the Sun
The Hole Inside the Earth

Pack Ice in Arctic Circle

Contents

The vocabulary in this book is slightly harder than for The Mysterious Affair at Styles and The Secret Adversary. If you are not familiar with words like the following, you should try those books first: truthfulness, occupied, unimaginable, commenced, mechanism.

Chapter One

My name is Captain Robert Walton. I write this story from my family home in Geneva.
  Marlow, September, 1817

On July 31st, 1799, my ship was voyaging through the Arctic Circle. We were nearly surrounded by ice, only leaving my ship the water in which she floated. Our situation was dangerous, especially as we were compassed round by a very thick fog. We anchored, hoping that the atmosphere and weather would change.

About two o'clock the mist cleared away, and we saw vast and irregular plains of ice, which seemed to have no end. Some of my comrades groaned, and my own mind began to fill with worrying thoughts, when we saw something strange. We saw a sledge pulled by dogs, pass on towards the north, half a mile away: a man, but very tall, sat in the sledge, and guided the dogs. We watched the traveller with our telescopes, until he was lost among the jagged sheets of ice.

We watched in wonder, thinking we were hundreds of miles from any land, but this amazing sight seemed to tell us that we were not. Shut in, however, by ice, it was impossible to follow him.

About two hours after this, we heard waves, and before night the ice broke and freed our ship. We, however, remained anchored until the morning, fearing our ship might crash into any large block of loose ice. I made use of this time to rest for a few hours.

In the morning, however, as soon as it was light, I went up on deck, and found all the sailors busy on one side of the ship, talking to someone in the sea. It was, in fact, a sledge, like that we had seen before, which had drifted towards us in the night, on a large fragment of ice. Only one dog remained alive; but there was a human being within it, whom the sailors were telling to enter the ship. He was not, as the other traveller seemed to be, a savage inhabitant of some undiscovered island, but a European. When I appeared on deck, the ship's second-in-command said, "Here is our captain, and he will not allow you to perish on the open sea."

On seeing me, the stranger spoke to me in English, although with a foreign accent. "Before I come on board your vessel," said he, "will you have the kindness to tell me where you are going?"

You may understand my surprise on hearing such a question from a man close to destruction, and who I would have thought would not swap my vessel for all the wealth on earth. I replied, however, that we were on a voyage of discovery towards the North Pole.

Upon hearing this he seemed satisfied, and agreed to come on board. Good God! If you had seen the man, your surprise would have been endless. His limbs were nearly frozen, and his body a bag of bones by tiredness and suffering. I never saw a man in so bad a condition. We attempted to carry him into the cabin; but as soon as he had left the fresh air, he fainted. We brought him back to the deck, and revived him by rubbing him with brandy, and forcing him to swallow a small quantity. As soon as he showed signs of life, we wrapped him up in blankets, and placed him near the chimney of the kitchen-stove. By slow degrees he recovered, and ate a little soup, which restored him wonderfully.

In the days that followed, my guest gradually came back to health. I learned that his name was Victor Frankenstein, and he told me the most incredible story. What follows is what he told me.

Chapter Two

My name is Victor Frankenstein. I am by birth a Genevese; and my family is one of the most famous of that republic. My ancestors had been for many years, government officials; and my father had filled several public positions with honour and good reputation. He was respected by all who knew him for his truthfulness and close attention to public business. He passed his younger days occupied by the affairs of his country; and it was not until the decline of life that he thought of marrying, and having sons who live up to his reputation.

Of these I was the eldest, and his heir. Nobody could have more tender parents than mine. My education and health were their constant care, especially as I remained for several years their only child. But before I continue my story, I must record an incident which took place when I was four years of age.

My father had a sister, whom he tenderly loved, and who had married early in life an Italian gentleman. Soon after her marriage, she had gone with her husband into her native country, and for years my father heard very little from her. About the time I mentioned she died; and a few months afterwards he received a letter from her husband, acquainting him with his intention of marrying an Italian lady, and requesting my father to take charge of his daughter, Elizabeth. "It is my wish," he said, "that you should consider her as your own daughter, and educate her. Her mother's fortune is given to her."

My father did not hesitate and immediately went to Italy, so that he might accompany the little Elizabeth to her future home. I have often heard my mother say that she was at that time the most beautiful child she had ever seen, and showed signs even then of a gentle and affectionate nature. These indications, and a desire to bind as closely as possible the ties of domestic love, convinced my mother to consider Elizabeth as my future wife; a plan which she never found reason to regret.

From this time Elizabeth Lavenza became my playmate, and, as we grew older, my friend. She was docile and good tempered, yet gay and playful as a summer insect. Although she was lively, her feelings were strong and deep, and her character unusually affectionate. No one could better enjoy freedom, yet no one could submit with more grace than she did to strict rules. Her imagination was great, yet her ability to focus was amazing. Her appearance was the image of her mind; her hazel eyes, although as lively as a bird's possessed an attractive softness. Her figure was light and airy; and, though capable of enduring great tiredness, she appeared the most fragile creature in the world. While I admired her understanding and fancy, I loved to tend on her, as I should on a favourite animal; and I never saw so much grace both of person and mind united to such honesty.

Everyone loved Elizabeth. We called each other familiarly by the name of cousin. No word, no expression could explain the kind of relation in which she stood to me—my more than sister, since till death she was to be mine only.

Geneva - 1860

Chapter Three

Elizabeth and I were brought up together; there being almost a year difference in our ages. On the birth of a second son, my junior by seven years, my parents gave up entirely their wandering life and fixed themselves in their native country. We possessed a house in Geneva, and another where we mostly lived, on the eastern shore of Geneva's lake, more than a mile from the city. I only had one close friend at school. Henry Clerval was the son of a merchant of Geneva. He was a boy of talent, loving work, hardship, and even danger for its own sake. He read many books, including tales of the Round Table of King Arthur.

When I was seventeen my parents decided that I should become a student at the university of Ingolstadt. My departure was therefore fixed at an early date, but before the day arrived, the first disaster of my life occurred—a sign of misery to come.

Elizabeth caught scarlet fever, and she was in the greatest danger. During her illness my mother attended her sickbed. Elizabeth was saved, but the consequences of my mother's care were fatal. On the third day my mother sickened; her fever was accompanied by the most alarming symptoms, making the doctors fear the worst. On her deathbed she joined the hands of Elizabeth and myself. "My children," she said, "my firmest hopes of future happiness were placed on the prospect of your marriage. This will now be the consolation of your father. Elizabeth, my love, you must supply my place to my younger children. Alas! I regret that I am taken from you; and, happy and beloved as I have been, is it not hard to quit you all? I will try to resign myself cheerfully to death and will hope of meeting you in another world." She died calmly, and her face expressed affection even in death. I need not describe the feelings of those whose dearest ties are torn by that most terrible evil and the despair that is shown on the face. It is so long before the mind can persuade itself that she whom we saw every day and whose very existence appeared a part of our own can have departed for ever. These are the reflections of the first days; but when the passing of time proves the reality of the evil, then the actual bitterness of grief commences.

Shortly after, I said my farewells to Elizabeth and my friend Clerval and left for my university and took up residence in my lonely apartment. The next morning, I paid a visit to some of the professors. Chance—or rather evil influence, the Angel of Destruction—led me first to M. Krempe, professor of physics. He was a rude man, but wise in the secrets of his science. He asked me several questions about my progress in the different branches of science similar to physics. I replied carelessly and mentioned the names of authors of books about magic I had studied. The professor stared.

"Have you," he said, "really spent your time studying such nonsense?"

I replied, "Yes."

"Every minute," continued M. Krempe with warmth, "every instant that you have wasted on those books is utterly and entirely lost. You have burdened your memory with exploded systems and useless names. Good God! In what desert have you lived, where no one was kind enough to inform you that these fantasies which you have so greedily digested are a thousand years old and as musty as they are ancient? I little expected, in this enlightened and scientific age, to find a disciple of Albertus Magnus and Paracelsus. My dear sir, you must begin your studies again."

So saying, he stepped aside and wrote down a list of several books treating of natural philosophy which he wanted me to read, and dismissed me after mentioning that in the beginning of the following week he intended to commence a course of lectures upon physics in its general relations, and that M. Waldman, a fellow professor, would lecture upon chemistry the alternate days that he omitted. I returned home not disappointed, for I have said that I had long considered those authors useless whom the professor reprobated; but I returned not at all the more inclined to recur to these studies in any shape. M. Krempe was a little squat man with a gruff voice and an ugly face; the teacher, therefore, did not impress me with his opinions. I intended to continue studying the magicians of old, because I felt that modern physics lacked the big ideas and ambitions of ancient times.

M. Waldman was very unlike his colleague. He appeared about fifty years old, but with a very kind face; a few grey hairs covered his temples, but those at the back of his head were nearly black and he had the sweetest voice I ever heard. He quietly explained that chemistry was in one way opposite to physics; in ancient times chemists achieved nothing, but in the modern world they could achieve miracles. His words excited me enormously. So much has been done, exclaimed the soul of Frankenstein—more, far more, will I achieve; treading in the steps already marked, I will pioneer a new way, explore unknown powers, and unfold to the world the deepest mysteries of creation.

The following morning, I visited M. Waldman and explained my ambitions. He told me that he believed I would achieve wonders as long as I studied *all* sciences, including mathematics.

He then took me into his laboratory and explained to me the uses of his various machines, instructing me as to what I ought to buy and promising me the use of his own when I should have advanced far enough in the science not to damage their mechanisms. He also gave me the list of books which I had requested, and I took my leave.

Chapter Four

My effort was at first uncertain; it gained strength as I proceeded and I soon became so eager that the stars often disappeared in the light of morning whilst I was still busy in my laboratory. Two years passed in this way, during which I never went home but was engaged, heart and soul, in the pursuit of some discoveries which I hoped to make.

When I had become as well acquainted with the theory and practice of physics as any of the professors at Ingolstadt and my stay no longer seemed necessary, I thought of returning to my friends and my native town, when an incident happened that delayed my departure.

One of the things which had attracted my attention was the structure of the human body, and, indeed, any animal. From where, I often asked myself, did the spark of life come? It was a bold question, and one which has always been considered as a mystery; yet how many things are we on the verge of discovering, if cowardice or carelessness do not hold us back. I considered these thoughts in my mind and decided to focus on physics to find the answer.

My father had taught me not to fear death and decay and, indeed, said that its study was necessary in any field of science. Darkness had no effect upon my imagination, and a churchyard was to me merely the receptacle of bodies deprived of life, which, from being beautiful and strong had become food for the worm. Now I had to examine the cause and progress of this process. My attention fixed upon every ugly horror of death that I could think of. I saw how the fine form of man was degraded and wasted; I saw how the corruption of death replaced the blooming cheek of life.

From the depth of this darkness a sudden light broke in upon me—a light so brilliant and wondrous, yet so simple, that while I became dizzy with the immensity of the idea which it illustrated, I was surprised that among so many men of genius who had studied the same science that I alone should be chosen to discover so astonishing a secret.

Remember, I am not recording the thoughts of a madman. The sun shining in the sky is not more certain that what I now know is true. Some miracle might have produced it, yet the stages of the discovery were distinct and probable. After days and nights of incredible labour and fatigue, I succeeded in discovering the cause of life; no, more, I became myself capable of making dead things live. What had been the study and desire of the wisest men since the creation of the world was now within my grasp.

I see by your eagerness and the wonder and hope which your eyes express, my friend, that you expect to be told of my secret; that cannot be; listen patiently until the end of my story, and you will easily see why I am silent upon that subject. I will not lead you on to your destruction and misery. Learn from me, if not by my morals, at least by my example, how dangerous knowledge can be and how much happier is the man who believes his native town to be the world than he who tries to become greater than his character will allow.

When I found this amazing power placed within my hands, I hesitated a long time about what I should do about it. Although I had the ability to give life, yet to prepare a body for it, with all its complex fibres, muscles, and veins, still remained a work of unimaginable difficulty and labour. I doubted at first whether I should attempt the creation of a human like myself, or a simpler one, but my imagination was too excited by my first success to doubt my ability to give life to an animal as complex and wonderful as man. The materials within my command hardly appeared enough to so tough a job, but I didn't doubt that I would succeed.

As the small size of the parts would slow me down, I decided to make the man of a gigantic size, that is to say, about eight feet tall. After this decision and having spent some months in successfully collecting and arranging my materials, I began.

In a lonely chamber, or rather cell, at the top of the house, and separated from all the other apartments by a gallery and staircase, I kept my workshop of filthy creation; my eyeballs were jumping from their sockets at the details of my work. The university biology room and the slaughter-house furnished many of my materials, and often I turned away with loathing from my work, whilst, still urged on by an eagerness which always increased, I brought my work near to an end.

The summer months passed while I continued, heart and soul, in one aim. It was a most beautiful season; never did the fields produce a better harvest or the vines yield a more crop of grapes, but my eyes were blind to the charms of nature.

Mont Blanc - Near Geneva

Chapter Five

It was on a dreary night of November that I saw the result of my toil. With an anxiety that almost amounted to agony, I collected the instruments of life around me, that I might place a spark of being into the lifeless thing that lay at my feet. It was already one in the morning; the rain pattered against the windowpanes, and my candle was nearly burnt out, when, by the glimmer of the half-light, I saw the dull, yellow eye of the creature open; it breathed hard, and a fit shook its limbs. How can I describe my emotions at this disaster, or how describe the wretch whom I had laboured to form?

His limbs were in proportion, and I had selected his features as beautiful. Beautiful! Great God! His yellow skin scarcely covered the work of muscles and arteries beneath; his hair was of a shiny black, and flowing; his teeth of a pearly whiteness; but these features only formed a more horrid contrast with his watery eyes that seemed almost of the same colour as the brown-white sockets in which they were set, his shrivelled complexion and straight black lips.

I had worked hard for nearly two years, for the sole purpose of placing life into a dead body. For this I had denied myself rest and health. I had desired it with a passion, but now that I had finished, the beauty of the dream vanished, and breathless horror and disgust filled my heart. Unable to endure the sight of the being I had created, I rushed out of the room and continued for a long time pacing my bed-chamber, unable to sleep.

But I had the most terrible dream. I thought I saw Elizabeth, in the bloom of health, walking in the streets of Ingolstadt. Delighted and surprised, I embraced her, but as I placed the first kiss on her lips, they became pale with the hue of death; her features appeared to change, and I thought that I held the corpse of my dead mother in my arms; a shroud covered her form, and I saw the grave-worms crawling in the folds of the flannel.

I awoke from my sleep with horror; a cold dew covered my forehead, my teeth chattered, and every limb shook, when, by the dim and yellow light of the moon, as it forced its way through the window shutters, I saw the wretch—the miserable monster whom I had created. He held up the curtain of the bed; and his eyes, if eyes they may be called, were fixed on me. His jaws opened, and he muttered some mumbling sounds, while a grin wrinkled his cheeks. He might have spoken, but I did not hear; one hand was stretched out, seemingly to detain me, but I escaped and rushed downstairs. I took refuge in the court-yard belonging to the house, where I remained during the rest of the night, walking up and down in the greatest confusion, listening carefully, catching and fearing each sound as if it were to announce the approach of the evil corpse to which I had so miserably given life.

Morning, dismal and wet, at length dawned. I went into the streets, pacing them with quick steps, as if I sought to avoid the wretch whom I feared every turning of the street would present to my view. I did not dare return to the apartment which I inhabited, but felt the need to hurry on, although drenched by the rain which poured from a black and comfortless sky.

Continuing thus, I came at length opposite to the inn at which the various carriages usually stopped. Here I paused, I knew not why; but I remained some minutes with my eyes fixed on a coach that was coming towards me from the other end of the street. As it drew nearer I observed that it was the Swiss caution; it stopped just where I was standing, and on the door being opened, I saw Henry Clerval, who, on seeing me, instantly sprung out.

"My dear Frankenstein," exclaimed, "I have persuaded my father to pay for my studies at the University. How glad I am to see you! How fortunate that you should be here at the very moment of my alighting!"

"Frankenstein! I have found you without even trying. I am so glad to find you well!"

"It gives me the greatest delight to see you; but tell me how you left my father, brothers, and Elizabeth."

"Very well, and very happy, only a little uneasy that they hear from you so seldom. But my dear Frankenstein … ." He, stopping short and gazing full in my face, continued, "I did not before say how very ill you appear; so thin and pale; you look as if you had been awake for several nights."

"You have guessed right; I have lately been so deeply involved in one task that I have not allowed myself sufficient rest, as you see; but I hope, I sincerely hope, that all these tasks are now at an end and that I am at length free."

I trembled excessively; I could not endure to think of, and far less to allude to, the events of the preceding night. I walked with a quick pace, and we soon arrived at my college. I then reflected, and the thought made me shiver, that the creature whom I had left in my apartment might still be there, alive and walking about. I dreaded to behold this monster, but I feared still more that Henry should see him. Asking him, therefore, to remain a few minutes at the bottom of the stairs, I darted up towards my own room. My hand was already on the lock of the door before I got a grip on myself. I then paused, and a cold shiver came over me. I threw the door open, as children do when they expect a ghost to stand in waiting for them on the other side; but nothing appeared. I stepped fearfully in: the apartment was empty, and my bedroom was also freed from its hideous guest. I could hardly believe that so great a good fortune could have befallen me, but when I became assured that my enemy had indeed fled, I clapped my hands for joy and ran down to Clerval.

We went up into my room, and the servant presently brought breakfast; but I was unable to contain myself. It was not joy only that possessed me; I felt my flesh tingle and my pulse beat rapidly. I was unable to sit still; I jumped over the chairs, clapped my hands, and laughed aloud. Clerval at first put down my joy on his arrival, but when he observed me more closely, he saw a wildness in my eyes which he couldn't explain, and my loud, heartless laughter frightened and astonished him.

"My dear Victor," cried he, "what, for God's sake, is the matter? Do not laugh in that manner. How ill you are! What is the cause of all this?"

"Do not ask me," cried I, putting my hands before my eyes, for I thought I saw the dreaded ghost glide into the room; "He can tell. Oh, save me! Save me!" I imagined that the monster seized me; I struggled furiously and fell down in a fit.

Poor Clerval! What must he have felt? A meeting, which he anticipated with such joy, so strangely turned to bitterness. But I did not see his grief, because I was lifeless and did not recover my senses for a long, long time. This was the beginning of a fever which kept me in the apartment for several months. During all that time Henry was my only nurse, concealing my illness from my family for fear that the long journey to Ingolstadt would kill my father.

I was very ill, and surely nothing but the endless care of my friend could have cured me. The form of the monster on whom I had given life was always before my eyes, and I raved about him. Doubtless my words surprised Henry; he at first believed them to be the ranting of my disturbed imagination, but the determination with which I continually recurred to the same subject persuaded him that my illness owed its origin to some unusual and terrible event.

By Spring, I began to recover. I became as cheerful as before I was attacked by the fatal passion.

"Dearest Clerval," exclaimed I, "how kind, how very good you are to me. This whole winter, instead of being spent in study, as you promised yourself, has been consumed in my sick room. How shall I ever repay you?"

"Write to your family. I have here a letter for you from Elizabeth. Tell them that you are well. That is all I ask!"

Chapter Six

I read the letter from Elizabeth.

My dearest Cousin,
You have been ill, very ill, and even the constant
letters of dear kind Henry are not sufficient to reassure me. You are unable to write—to hold a pen;
yet one word from you, dear Victor, is necessary to
calm our worries. For a long time, I have thought
that each post would bring this line, and I have
managed to dissuade my uncle from undertaking a
journey to Ingolstadt, yet how often have I regretted
not being able to perform it myself! I figure to myself that the task of attending on your sickbed has
been placed upon some cruel old nurse, who could
never guess your wishes nor attend to them with the
care and affection of your poor cousin. Yet that is
over now: Clerval writes that indeed you are getting
better. I eagerly hope that you will confirm this
news soon in your own handwriting. Get well—and
return to us. You will find a happy, cheerful home
and friends who love you dearly. Your father's
health is good, and he asks not to see you, but to be
assured that you are well; and that not a worry will
ever cloud his happy face.
I have written myself into better spirits, dear cousin;
but my anxiety returns to me as I conclude. Write,
dearest Victor,—one line—one word will be a
blessing to us. Ten thousand thanks to Henry for his
kindness, his affection, and his many letters; we are
sincerely grateful. Goodbye! my cousin; take care
of yourself; and, I entreat you, write!
Elizabeth Lavenza. Geneva, March 18th.

"Dear, dear Elizabeth!" I exclaimed, when I had read her letter: "I will write instantly and relieve them from the anxiety they must feel." I wrote, and this exertion greatly tired me; but my healing had commenced, and proceeded regularly. In another fortnight I was able to leave my chamber.

When I was healthy again, the sight of a chemical instrument would renew all the agony of my illness. Henry saw this, and had removed all my apparatus from my view. He had also changed my apartment; for he saw that I had acquired a dislike for the room which had previously been my laboratory. He urged me to return to Geneva for a holiday, and I agreed.

Summer passed, and my return to Geneva was fixed for the latter end of autumn; but being delayed by several accidents, winter and snow arrived, the roads were deemed impassable, and my journey was delayed until the following spring. I felt this delay very bitterly, because I longed to see my native town and my beloved friends. My return had only been delayed so long from an unwillingness to leave Clerval in a strange place, before he had become acquainted with any of its inhabitants. The winter, however, was spent cheerfully; and although the spring was unusually late, when it came its beauty compensated for its lateness.

Before I returned home, Clerval suggesting a hike into the mountains. I was fond of exercise, and Clerval had always been my favourite companion in the rambles of this kind that I had taken among the scenes of my native country. We returned to our college on a Sunday afternoon: the peasants were dancing, and every one we met appeared gay and happy. My own spirits were high, and I ran along with feelings of unbridled joy.

Chapter Seven

On my return, I found the following letter from my father:—

My dear Victor,

You have probably waited impatiently for a letter to fix the date of your return to us; and I was at first tempted to write only a few lines, merely mentioning the day on which I should expect you. But that would be a cruel kindness, and I dare not do it. What would be your surprise, my son, when you expected a happy and glad welcome, to see tears and misery? And how, Victor, can I explain our misfortune?

Your youngest brother, William, is dead!—that sweet child, whose smiles delighted and warmed my heart, who was so gentle, yet so gay! Victor, he is murdered! I will not attempt to console you; but will simply explain the circumstances of his death.

Last Thursday (May 7th), I, my niece, and your two brothers, went to walk in Plainpalais. The evening was warm and serene, and we extended our walk farther than usual. It was already dusk before we thought of returning; and then we discovered that William and Ernest, who had gone on before, were not to be found. We rested on a seat until they should return. Presently Ernest came, and enquired if we had seen his brother; he said, that he had been playing with him, that William had run away to hide himself, and that he vainly sought for him, and afterwards waited for a long time, but that he did not return. This account rather alarmed us, and we continued to search for him until night fell, when Elizabeth suggested that he might have returned to the house. He was not there. We returned again, with torches; for I could not rest, when I thought that my sweet boy had lost himself, and was exposed to all the damps and dews of night; Elizabeth also suffered extreme anguish. About five in the morning I discovered my lovely boy, whom the night before I had seen blooming and active in health, stretched on the grass livid and motionless; the print of the murder's finger was on his neck.

He was carried home, and the anguish that was visible in my face revealed the secret to Elizabeth. She was very keen to see the corpse. At first, I attempted to prevent her, but she persisted, and entering the room where it lay, hastily examined the neck of the victim, and clasping her hands exclaimed

"O God! I have murdered my darling child!"

She fainted, and was revived with extreme difficulty. When she was awake, it was only to weep and sigh. She told me, that that same evening William had teased her to let him wear a very valuable portrait pendant that she possessed of your mother. This picture is gone, and was doubtless the temptation which urged the murderer to the deed.

We have no trace of him at present, although our attempts to discover him are unfinished; but they will not restore my beloved William! Come, dearest Victor; you alone can console Elizabeth. She weeps continually, and accuses herself unjustly to be the cause of his death; her words pierce my heart. We are all unhappy; but will not that be an additional motive for you, my son, to return and be our comforter? Alas, Victor!

Your affectionate and afflicted father,
Alphonse Frankenstein. Geneva, May 12th.

Henry, when he saw me weep with bitterness, asked:
"Are you always to be unhappy? My dear friend, what has happened?"

I handed him the letter and watched him read it with a pained expression on his face.

"I can offer you no comfort, my friend," said he; "your disaster is terrible. What do you intend to do?"

"To go instantly to Geneva: come with me to the stables, Henry, to order the horses."

My journey was very sad. At first, I wished to hurry on, for I longed to console and sympathise with my loved and sorrowing friends; but when I drew near my native town, I slackened my progress. I could hardly contain the multitude of feelings that crowded into my mind. I passed through scenes familiar to my youth, but which I had not seen for nearly six years. Fear overcame me; I dared go no further for a while, dreading a thousand nameless evils that made me tremble, although I was unable to define them.

It was completely dark when I arrived in Geneva; the gates of the town were already shut; and I was obliged to pass the night at Secheron, a village at the distance of half a league from the city. The sky was serene; and, as I was unable to rest, I resolved to visit the spot where my poor William had been murdered. As I could not pass through the town, I had to cross the lake in a boat to arrive at Plainpalais. During this short voyage I saw the lightning playing on the summit of Mont Blanc in the most beautiful figures. The storm appeared to approach rapidly, and, on landing, I climbed a low hill, that I might observe its progress. It advanced; the heavens were clouded, and I soon felt the rain coming slowly in large drops, but its violence quickly increased. I left my seat, and walked on, although the darkness and storm increased every minute, and the thunder burst with a terrific crash over my head. It was echoed from Salêve, the Juras, and the Alps of Savoy; vivid flashes of lightning dazzled my eyes, illuminating the lake, making it appear like a vast sheet of fire; then for an instant everything seemed of a pitch blackness, until the eye recovered itself from the last flash.

This noble war in the sky elevated my spirits; I clasped my hands, and exclaimed aloud, "William, dear angel! this is thy funeral, this thy dirge!" As I said these words, I saw in the gloom a figure which stole from behind a clump of trees near me; I stood fixed, gazing intently: I could not be mistaken. A flash of lightning illuminated the object, and revealed its shape plainly to me; its gigantic size, and the deformity of its shape more hideous than any human, instantly informed me that it was the filthy demon, to whom I had given life. What was he doing there? Could he be the murderer of my brother? No sooner did that idea cross my mind, than I became convinced of its truth; my teeth chattered, and I was forced to lean against a tree for support. The figure passed me quickly, and I lost it in the gloom. Nothing in human shape could have destroyed the fair child. He was the murderer! I could not doubt it.

No one can understand the anguish I suffered during the remainder of the night, which I spent, cold and wet, in the open air. But I did not feel the bad weather; my imagination was busy in scenes of evil and despair. I considered the being whom I had created, a creature given the will and power to commit horrors, such as the deed which he had now done, nearly in the light of my own vampire, my own spirit let loose from the grave, and forced to destroy all that was dear to me. Day dawned; and I walked towards the town. The gates were open, and I hastened to my father's house. My first thought was to discover what I knew of the murderer, and instantly chase him. But I paused when I thought about the story that I had to tell.

Chapter Eight

It was about five in the morning when I entered my father's house. I told the servants not to disturb the family, and went into the library to wait for them to wake.

My brother, Ernest, arrived first and told me that they had found the murderer, a woman called Justine Moritz!

"Justine Moritz! Poor, poor girl, is she the accused? But it is wrongfully; everyone knows that; no one believes it, surely, Ernest?"

"No one did at first; but several factors came out, that have almost forced the belief upon us, and her own behaviour has been so confused us that it has added to the evidence of facts that leave no doubt. But she will be tried today, and you will then hear all."

He then told us that, the morning on which the murder of poor William had been discovered, Justine had been taken ill, and confined to her bed for several days. During this time, one of the servants, happening to examine the clothes she had worn on the night of the murder, had discovered in her pocket the picture of my mother, which had been judged to be the temptation of the murderer. The servant instantly showed it to one of the others, who, without saying a word to any of the family, went to a lawyer; and, upon their statement to the court, Justine was arrested. On being charged with the fact, the poor girl confirmed the suspicion by her extreme confusion.

This was a strange tale, but it did not shake my faith, and I replied seriously:

"You are all mistaken; I know the murderer. Justine, poor, good Justine, is innocent."

We were soon joined by Elizabeth. Time had altered her since I last beheld her; it had given her loveliness beyond the beauty of her childhood. There was the same openness, the same sense of fun, but it was now joined to an expression of sensitivity and intelligence. She welcomed me with the greatest affection.

"Your arrival, my dear cousin," said she, "fills me with hope. You perhaps will find some means to justify my poor, innocent Justine. Alas! who is safe if she is convicted of crime today? I rely on her innocence as certainly as I do upon my own. Our bad luck is doubly hard to us; we have not only lost that lovely darling boy, but this poor girl, whom I sincerely love, is to be torn away by an even worse fate. If she is condemned, I never shall know joy more. But she will not, I am sure she will not, and then I shall be happy again, even after the sad death of my little William."

"She is innocent, my Elizabeth," said I, "and that shall be proved; fear nothing, but let your spirits be cheered by the certainty of her release."

Portrait Locket

Chapter Nine

We passed a few, sad hours until eleven o'clock, when Justine's trial was to commence. My father and the rest of the family having to attend as witnesses, I went with them to the court. During the whole of this wretched mockery of justice I suffered living torture. I could not endure the horror of my situation, and when I saw that the faces of the jury and the judges had already condemned Justine, I rushed out of the court in agony. The tortures of the accused did not equal mine; she was strengthened by innocence, but the fangs of remorse tore my bosom and would not let go their hold.

I passed a night of wretchedness. In the morning I went to the court; my lips and throat were dry. I dared not ask the fatal question, but I was known, and the officer guessed the cause of my visit. The jury had ruled, and Justine was condemned.

The person to whom I addressed myself added that Justine had already confessed her guilt.

I hastened to return home, and Elizabeth eagerly demanded the result. Upon my reply she insisted we return to the court together, where she learned that Justine had confessed under pressure. I gnashed my teeth and ground them together, uttering a groan that came from my innermost soul when we reached Justine's cell. She started. When she saw who it was, she approached me and said:

"Dear sir, you are very kind to visit me; you, I hope, do not believe that I am guilty?"

I could not answer.

"No, Justine," said Elizabeth; "he is more convinced of your innocence than I was, for even when he heard that you had confessed, he did not credit it."

Justine gathered her wits and in a defiant voice cried:

"Farewell, sweet lady, dearest Elizabeth, my beloved and only friend; may heaven, in its bounty, bless and preserve you; may this be the last misfortune that you will ever suffer! Live, and be happy, and make others so."

And the next day Justine died.

Chapter Ten

It was during an access of this kind that I suddenly left my home, and trekking to the nearby Alpine valleys, sought in their magnificence, the eternity of such scenes, to forget myself and my sorrows. My feet were directed towards the valley of Chamounix. I had visited it frequently during my boyhood.

I spent the following day roaming through the valley. I stood beside the sources of the River Arveiron, whose source is a glacier that with slow pace is advancing down from the summit of the hills to barricade the valley.

The day had started bright and sunny, but clouds crept over the horizon, and before long I became drenched in a rain, a flood, that would not stop. I turned back for Chamounix, but became lost and found myself on a glacier. The field of ice is almost a league in width, but I spent nearly two hours in crossing it, reaching at last the mountain on the opposite side of the ice sheet.

I suddenly beheld the figure of a man, at some distance, advancing towards me with superhuman speed. He bounded over the crevices in the ice, among which I had walked with caution; his height, also, as he approached, seemed to exceed that of man. I was troubled; a mist came over my eyes, and I felt a faintness seize me, but I was quickly restored by the cold gale of the mountains. I perceived, as the shape came nearer, that it was the wretch whom I had created. I trembled with rage and horror, deciding to wait for his approach and then meet him in mortal combat.

"Devil," I exclaimed, "do you dare approach me? And do not you fear the fierce revenge of my fist on your miserable head?"

"I expected this reception," said the demon. "All men hate the wretched; how, then, must I be hated, who am miserable beyond all living things! Yet you, my creator, detest and spurn me, thy creature, to whom you are bound by ties that only can be broken by the destruction of one of us. You want to kill me. How dare you meddle thus with life? Do your duty towards me, and I will do mine towards you and the rest of mankind. If you will comply with my wishes, I will leave them and you at peace, but if you refuse, I will fill the mouth of death, until it be satisfied with the blood of your remaining friends."

"Disgusting monster! The tortures of hell are too mild a revenge for your crimes. Wretched devil! You accuse me for creating you, come on, then, that I may blow out the spark which I so stupidly created."

My rage was unlimited; I sprang on him, driven by all the feelings which can arm one human against the existence of another.

He easily eluded me and said:

"Be calm! I ask you to hear me before you give vent to your hatred on my soul. Oh, Frankenstein, be not the same as everyone else and trample upon me alone, to whom your justice, and even affection, is most due. Remember that I am your creature; I ought to be thy Adam of the Bible, but I am rather the fallen angel, Lucifer, whom you drive from joy for no reason. Everywhere I see bliss, from which I alone am always excluded. I was always good; only misery made me a fiend. Make me happy, and I shall again be virtuous."

"Begone! I will not hear you."

"Let your compassion be moved, and do not reject me. Listen to my tale; when you have heard that, abandon or reward me, as I deserve. But hear me. The guilty are allowed, by human laws, bloody as they are, to speak in their own defence before they are condemned. Listen to me, Frankenstein. You accuse me of murder, and yet you would, with a satisfied conscience, destroy your own creature. Oh, praise the eternal justice of man! Yet I ask you not to spare me; listen to me, and then, if you can, and if you will, destroy the work of your hands."

As he said this he led the way across the ice; I followed.

I had until now supposed him to be the murderer of my brother, and I eagerly sought a confirmation or denial of this opinion. For the first time, also, I felt what the duties of a creator towards his creature were, and that I ought to make him happy before I complained of his wickedness. These motives urged me to comply with his demand. We crossed the ice, therefore, and ascended the opposite rock. The air was cold, and the rain again began to descend; we entered the hut, the fiend looking satisfied, I with a heavy heart and depressed spirits. But I agreed to listen, and seating myself by the fire which my companion had lighted, he thus began his tale. This is what he told me.

Valley of Chamonix

Chapter Eleven

It was dark when I first awoke in your laboratory; I felt cold and half frightened, finding myself so desolate. Before I quitted your apartment, on a feeling of cold, I had covered myself with some clothes, but these were not enough to secure me from the dews of night. I was a poor, helpless, miserable wretch; I knew, and could distinguish, nothing; but feeling pain invade me on all sides, I sat down and wept. Soon a gentle light stole over the heavens and gave me a feeling of pleasure. I started up and beheld a radiant form rise from among the trees. The moon I gazed at with a kind of wonder. It moved slowly, but it lit my path, and I went out in search of berries, which I had found good to eat. I was still cold when under one of the trees I found a huge cloak, with which I covered myself and sat down upon the ground. No distinct ideas occupied my mind; all was confused. I felt light, and hunger, and thirst, and darkness; numerous sounds rang in my ears, and on all sides various scents reached my nose; the only object that I could distinguish was the bright moon, and I fixed my eyes on that with pleasure.

One day, when I was depressed by cold, I found a fire which had been left by some wandering beggars, and was overcome with delight at the warmth I experienced from it. In my joy I thrust my hand into the live embers, but quickly drew it out again with a cry of pain. How strange, I thought, that the same cause should produce such opposite effects! I examined the materials of the fire, and to my joy found it to be composed of wood. I quickly collected some branches, but they were wet and would not burn. I was pained at this and sat still watching the operation of the fire. The wet wood which I had placed near the heat dried and itself became inflamed. I reflected on this, and by touching the various branches, I discovered the cause and busied myself in collecting a great quantity of wood, that I might dry it and have a plentiful supply of fire.

I soon became hungry, however, and had to seek something to eat. I began to walk, and at length I perceived a small hut, on a rising ground, which had doubtless been built for the convenience of some shepherd. This was a new sight to me, and I examined the structure with great curiosity. Finding the door open, I entered. An old man sat in it, near a fire, over which he was preparing his breakfast. He turned on hearing a noise, and perceiving me, shrieked loudly, and quitting the hut, ran across the fields with a speed of which his age hardly appeared capable. His appearance, different from any I had ever before seen, and his flight somewhat surprised me. But I was enchanted by the appearance of the hut; here the snow and rain could not enter. I greedily ate the remains of the shepherd's breakfast, which consisted of bread, cheese, milk, and wine; the latter, however, I did not like. Then, overcome by tiredness, I lay down among some straw and fell asleep.

It was noon when I awoke, and allured by the warmth of the sun, which shone brightly on the white ground, I decided to continue my travels; and, packing the remains of the peasant's breakfast in a wallet I found, I proceeded across the fields for several hours, until at sunset I arrived at a village. How miraculous did this appear! I admired the huts, the neater cottages, and stately houses. The vegetables in the gardens, the milk and cheese that I saw placed at the windows of some of the cottages, tempted me. One of the best of these I entered, but I had hardly placed my foot within the door before the children shrieked, and one of the women fainted. The whole village was roused; some fled, some attacked me, until, bruised by stones and many other kinds of missile weapons, I escaped to the open country and fearfully took refuge in a low hut, quite bare, and making a wretched appearance after the palaces I had beheld in the village. This

hut however, joined a cottage of a neat and pleasant appearance, but after my previous experience, I dared not
enter it. My place of refuge was constructed of wood, but
so low that I could with difficulty sit upright in it. No
wood, however, was placed on the earth, which formed
the floor, but it was dry; and although the wind entered it
by innumerable chinks, I found it a refuge from the snow
and rain.

Shepherd's Cottage in Alps

Chapter Twelve

I survived by stealing bread from the cottage, when its occupants were out, and water from a nearby stream. But my curiosity about the three people that provided my food became too great to ignore. I had already seen a young man and woman enter and leave the cottage and heard the cracked voice of somebody else within, as well as a sound I could not identify, so sweet that it made my heart soar with delight. One afternoon, as I heard them all in conversation within, I crept up to the cottage and peered through a chink in the wooden planks that sealed up the windows.

A small room, its walls whitewashed, lay before me furnished as barely as could be imagined.

I saw an old man, sitting in a chair, and the young girl say something to him, before she opened a drawer, pulled out something made of wood, with six strings stretched upon it, and began to pluck these. The sound made was sweeter than the song of the thrush or nightingale. For many days I continued to watch them through the chink. The gentle manners and beauty of the cottagers greatly endeared them to me; when they were unhappy, I felt depressed; when they rejoiced, I sympathised in their joys.

I began, by degrees, to understand that they communicated by making sounds with their mouths, and I practiced certain words they used regularly for each other, such as 'dear,' 'sister' and 'father.' It didn't take me long before I began to piece together whole sentences and learned to speak myself.

The young man most often spent time outside. Sometimes he set off for some nearby town and returned hours later. At other times he worked in the garden, but as there was little to do in the frosty season that now began, he read to the old man and the young woman. This reading had puzzled me extremely at first, but by degrees I discovered that he uttered many of the same sounds when he read as when he talked. I conjectured, therefore, that he found on the paper signs for speech which he understood, and I longed to understand these also.

I formed in my imagination a thousand pictures of presenting myself to them, and their reception of me. I imagined that they would be disgusted, until, by my gentle manners and soothing words, I should first win their favour and afterwards their love.

At night, however, I would often come to think of myself again as loathsome; I was not even of the same nature as man. I was more agile than they and could survive upon coarser diet; I bore the extremes of heat and cold with less injury to my body; my height far exceeded theirs. When I looked around I saw and heard of none like me. Was I, then, a monster, a blot upon the earth, from which all men fled and whom all men disowned? I cannot describe to you the agony that these thoughts brought upon me; I tried to ignore them, but sorrow only increased with knowledge. Oh, how I wished that I had never left my native wood, nor known nor felt beyond the feelings of hunger, thirst, and heat!

Chapter Thirteen

One night during my usual visit to the neighbouring wood where I collected my own food and brought home firewood that I left for my protectors as payment for bread, I found on the ground a leather suitcase containing several articles of dress and some books. I eagerly seized the prize and returned with it to my own hut. Fortunately, the books were written in the language, the elements of which I had acquired at the cottage; they consisted of Paradise Lost, a volume of Plutarch's Lives, and the Sorrows of Werter. The possession of these treasures gave me extreme delight; I now continually studied and exercised my mind upon these histories, whilst my friends were employed in their ordinary occupations. Soon after my return to the hovel I discovered some papers in the pocket of the dress which I had taken from your laboratory. I was aided by these papers that I had torn from your own notebook about my creation, labelled diagrams of which gave me a few words to begin with, such as 'heart,' 'head' and 'man.'

Later, I practised reading using your notes. You described in these papers every step you took in the progress of your work; this history was mingled with accounts of domestic events. You surely remember these papers. Here they are. Everything is related in them which bears reference to my origin. I sickened as I read. 'Hateful day when I received life!' I exclaimed in agony. 'Accursed creator! Why did you form a monster so hideous that even you turned from me in disgust? God, in pity, made man beautiful, but you made me filthy and hideous.

Chapter Fourteen

One day I saw my reflection in water and clawed at the stream in anguish. The sound of a young girl singing tore my eyes away from the water and I hid myself underneath a cypress tree. I watched as the girl ran, laughing, past me and reached the side of the stream. Her foot slipped, and she fell in. I rushed from my hiding place, and with extreme effort, saved her from the current and dragged her to the shore. I tried by every means I could think of to restore her to animation but was interrupted by the approach of a villager.

On seeing me, the man ran forward and grabbed the girl from my arms. He retreated, turned and ran, but I pursued him. He hadn't gone far when he realised he could not outrun me. Turning, he aimed the barrel of a small gun at me and fired! I sank to the ground, and my attacker escaped!

"This then is the reward for kindness!" I told myself.

I wept bitterly and crept away, gnashing my teeth the pain from torn muscle and smashed bone.

For some weeks I hung between life and death. The ball had entered my shoulder and remained there, but after a time the wound began to heal, and I continued my journey.

My toils now drew near a close; and, two months from this time, I reached Geneva. It was evening when I arrived, and I found a hiding-place among the fields that surround it, to meditate in what way I should approach you. I was disturbed by the approach of a beautiful child, who came running into the recess I had chosen. I thought that if I could seize him, and educate him as my companion and friend, I should not be so lonely on this earth.

Urged by this thought, I seized on the boy as he passed, and drew him towards me. As soon as he saw my form, he placed his hands before his eyes, and uttered a shrill scream: I drew his hand forcibly from his face, and said:

"Child, what is the meaning of this? I do not intend to hurt you: listen to me."

He struggled violently.

"Let me go," he cried. "Monster! ugly wretch! you wish to eat me, and tear me to pieces – You are an ogre – Let me go, or I will tell my papa."

"Frankenstein! you belong then to my enemy – to him towards whom I have sworn eternal revenge; you shall be my first victim."

The child still struggled, and pleaded for mercy. I grasped his throat to silence him, and in a moment, he lay dead at my feet. I gazed on my victim, and my heart swelled with hellish triumph: clapping my hands, I exclaimed:

"I, too, can create desolation; my enemy is not so strong! This death will carry despair to him, and a thousand other miseries shall torment and destroy him."

As I fixed my eyes on the child, I saw something glittering on his breast. I took it; it was a portrait of a most lovely woman. In spite of my foul mood, it softened and attracted me. For a few moments I gazed with delight on her dark eyes, fringed by deep lashes, and her lovely lips; but presently my rage returned: I remembered that I was for ever deprived of the delights that such beautiful creatures could bestow.

While I was overcome by these feelings, I left the spot where I had committed the murder, and was seeking a more secluded hiding-place, when I perceived a woman passing near me. She was young, not indeed so beautiful as her whose portrait I held, but of an agreeable appearance, and blooming in the loveliness of youth and health. Here, I thought, is one of those whose smiles are bestowed on all but me; she shall not escape; thanks to the lessons of the young man at the cottage, and the plain laws of man, I have learned how to work mischief. I approached her unseen, and placed the portrait securely in one of the folds of her dress.

For some days I haunted the spot where these scenes had taken place; sometimes wishing to see you, sometimes resolved to quit the world and its miseries for ever. At length I wandered towards these mountains, and have ranged through their immense peaks, consumed by a burning passion which you alone can gratify. We may not part until you have promised to comply with my need. I am alone, and miserable; man will not associate with me; but one as deformed and horrible as myself would not deny herself to me. My companion must be of the same species, and have the same defects. This being you must create.

Chapter Fifteen

The monster finished speaking, and fixed his looks upon me, expecting a reply. But I was shocked, confused, and unable to arrange my ideas sufficiently to understand the full extent of his request. He continued:

"You must create a female for me, with whom I can live in the exchange of those sympathies necessary for my being. This you alone can do; and I demand it of you as a right which you must not refuse."

"I do refuse it," I replied; "and no torture shall ever force me to agree. You may make me the most miserable of men, but you shall never make me disgusting in my own eyes. Shall I create another like yourself, whose joint wickedness might desolate the world. Begone! I have answered you; you may torture me, but I will never agree."

"You are in the wrong," replied the fiend; "and, instead of threatening, I am content to reason with you. I will revenge what you have done to me: if I cannot inspire love, I will cause fear; and chiefly towards you my enemy I swear hatred. Have a care: I will work at your destruction if you do not grant my wish. What I ask of you is reasonable and moderate; I demand a creature of another sex, but as hideous as myself: the pleasure is small, but it is all that I can receive, and it shall content me. It is true, we shall be monsters, cut off from all the world; but because of that we shall be more attached to one another. Our lives will not be happy, but they will be harmless, and free from the misery I now feel. Oh! my creator, make me happy; let me feel gratitude towards you for one benefit! Let me see that I excite the sympathy of some existing thing; do not deny me my request!"

I was moved. I shuddered when I thought of the possible results of my consent; but I felt that there was some justice in his argument. His tale, and the feelings he now expressed, proved him to be a creature of fine feelings; and did I not, as his maker, owe him all the portion of happiness that it was in my power to bestow?

He saw my change of feeling, and continued:

"If you consent, neither you nor any other human being shall ever see us again: I will go to the vast wilds of South America. My food is not that of man; I do not destroy the lamb and the kid, to satisfy my appetite; acorns and berries give me sufficient nourishment. I now see compassion in your eyes; let me seize the favourable moment, and persuade you to promise what I so passionately desire."

"You propose," replied I, "to fly from the habitations of man, to dwell in those wilds where the beasts of the field will be your only companions. How can you, who long for the love and sympathy of man, continue in this exile? You will return, and again seek their kindness, and you will meet with their disgust; your evil passions will be renewed, and you will then have a companion to aid you in the task of destruction. This cannot be; cease to argue the point, for I cannot agree."

"I will quit the neighbourhood of man, and dwell, as it may chance, in the most savage of places. My evil passions will have fled, for I shall meet with sympathy; my life will flow quietly away, and, in my dying moments, I shall not curse my maker."

His words had a strange effect upon me. I felt sorry for him, and sometimes felt a wish to console him; but when I looked upon him, when I saw what I created, I doubted my own powers of wisdom. I replied:

"I agree to your demand, on your solemn oath to quit Europe for ever, and every other place in the neighbourhood of man, as soon as I shall deliver into your hands a female who will accompany you in your exile." "I swear," he cried, "by the sun, and by the blue sky of heaven, that if you grant my prayer, while they exist you shall never see me again. Depart to your home, and commence your labours: I shall watch their progress with anxiety; and don't doubt that when you are ready I shall appear."

Saying this, he suddenly quitted me, fearful, perhaps, of any change in my mind. I saw him descend the mountain with greater speed than the flight of an eagle, and quickly lost him among the jagged peaks in the sea of ice. I exclaimed:

"Oh! stars, and clouds, and winds, ye are all about to mock me: if ye really pity me, crush feeling and memory; let me become nothing; but if not, depart, depart and leave me in darkness." These were wild and miserable thoughts; but I cannot describe to you how the eternal twinkling of the stars weighed upon me, and how I listened to every blast of wind, as if it were a dull, ugly desert wind on its way to consume me. Morning dawned before I arrived at the village of Chamounix; but my presence, so weary and strange, hardly calmed the fears of my family, who had waited the whole night in anxious expectation of my return.

The following day we returned to Geneva. The intention of my father in coming had been to divert my mind, and to restore me to my lost happiness; but the medicine had been fatal. And, unable to account for the misery I appeared to suffer, he hastened to return home, hoping the quiet of a domestic life would heal me from whatever cause it might spring.

I put off my return to my university, because I couldn't bear to think of the task ahead, but my father pulled me aside one day and said:

"I confess, my son, that I have always looked forward to your marriage with your cousin. You were attached to each other from your earliest infancy; you studied together, and appeared, in character and tastes, entirely suited to one another. But so blind is the experience of man, that what I thought to be the be my best idea may be the worst. You, perhaps, regard her as your sister, without any wish that she might become your wife. Nay, you may have met with another whom you may love; and, considering yourself as bound in honour to your cousin, this struggle may occasion the misery which you appear to feel."

"My dear father, reassure yourself. I love my cousin tenderly and sincerely. I never saw any woman who excited, as Elizabeth does, my warmest admiration and affection. My future hope is that we will, indeed, marry."

I could see where my father's argument led; he wished me to wed my cousin at once, but I could not commit to happiness until I had shed the burden of my debt to the creature. These feelings dictated my answer to my father. I expressed a wish to visit England; but, concealing the true reasons of this request, I clothed my desires under the disguise of wishing to travel and see the world before I sat down for life within the walls of my native town. I proposed this idea seriously, and my father was easily induced to comply. Our plan was soon arranged. I should travel to Strasburgh, where Clerval would join me. Some short time would be spent in the towns of Holland, and our principal stay would be in England. We should return by France; and it was agreed that the tour should occupy the space of two years. I agreed that I would wed Elizabeth upon my return.

For myself, I could not bear to leave my family so near the horror that I had created. But he had promised to follow me wherever I might go; and would he not accompany me to England? This imagination was dreadful in itself, but soothing, because it meant the safety of my friends. I was agonized with the idea of the possibility that the reverse of this might happen. But through the whole period during which I was the slave of my creature, I allowed myself to be governed by the impulses of the moment; and my present feelings strongly suggested that the fiend would follow me, and leave my family alone.

It was at the end of August that I departed, to pass two years of exile. Elizabeth approved of the reasons of my departure, and only regretted that she had not the same opportunities of enlarging her experience, and cultivating her understanding. She wept, however, as she bade me farewell, and pleaded with me to return happy. "We all," said she, "depend upon you; and if you are miserable, what must be our feelings?"

After some days spent in a comfortable carriage, during which I travelled many leagues, I arrived at Strasburgh, where I waited two days for Clerval. He came. Alas, how great was the contrast between us! He was alive to every new scene; joyful when he saw the beauties of the setting sun, and more happy when he beheld it rise, and begin a new day. He pointed out to me the shifting colours of the landscape, and the appearances of the sky.

We had agreed to descend the River Rhine in a boat from Strasburgh to Rotterdam, whence we might take a ship for London. It was on a clear morning, in the latter days of December, that I first saw the white cliffs of Britain. The banks of the Thames presented a new scene; they were flat, but fertile, and almost every town was marked by the remembrance of some story.

Chapter Sixteen

After passing some months in London, we received a letter from a person in Scotland, who had once been our visitor at Geneva. He mentioned the beauties of his native country, and asked us if we would extend our journey as far north as Perth, where he resided. Clerval eagerly desired to accept this invitation; and I, although I wanted to avoid people, wished to view again mountains and streams, and all the wondrous works with which Nature adorns her chosen dwelling-places.

We arrived at the Scottish town of Perth, where our friend awaited us. But I was in no mood to laugh and talk with strangers, or enter into their feelings or plans with the good humour expected from a guest; and so I told Clerval that I wished to make the tour of Scotland alone.

"You," said I, "enjoy yourself, and let this be our rendezvous. I may be absent a month or two; but do not interfere with my travels, I beg you: leave me in peace for a short time; and when I return, I hope it will be with a lighter heart."

Having parted from my friend, I decided to visit some remote spot of Scotland, and finish my work in solitude. I did not doubt that the monster followed me, and would reveal himself to me when I had finished. With this decision I crossed the northern highlands, and fixed on one of the remotest of the most northern British islands of the Orkneys as the scene for my work. It was a place fitted for such a work, being hardly more than a rock, whose high sides were continually beaten upon by the waves. The soil was barren, scarcely providing pasture for a few miserable cows, and oatmeal for its inhabitants, which consisted of five persons, whose gaunt and scraggy limbs gave indicated their miserable diet. Vegetables and bread, when they indulged in such luxuries, and even fresh water, were to be fetched from the main land, which was about five miles distant.

I hired one of the only three huts on the island and set to work. As I proceeded in my labour, it became every day more horrible to me. Sometimes I could not enter my laboratory for several days; and at other times I toiled day and night in order to complete my work. It was indeed a filthy process in which I was engaged. Every moment I feared to meet the monster. Sometimes I sat with my eyes fixed on the ground, fearing to raise them in case they should see the demon I had already created. I feared to wander from the sight of my fellow-creatures, in case he should come to claim his companion.

In the mean time I worked on, and my labour was already considerably advanced. I looked towards its completion with a tremulous and eager hope, mixed with fears of evil, that made my heart sicken in my bosom.

Chapter Seventeen

As I sat one night in my hut, I realised that if I created a female for my demon, there would be the possibility that I was creating a race of demons, a cursed people who would never find peace on Earth.

I trembled, and my heart failed within me; when, on looking up, I saw, by the light of the moon, the demon at the window. A ghastly grin wrinkled his lips as he gazed on me, where I sat fulfilling the task which he had allotted to me. Yes, he had followed me in my travels; he had hidden in forests, hid himself in caves, or taken refuge in wide and desert heaths; and he now came to check on my progress, and claim his reward.

As I looked on him, his face expressed the most terrible evil. I thought I had to be mad for creating another like to him, and, trembling with passion, tore to pieces the thing on the table. The wretch saw me destroy the creature on whose future existence he depended for happiness, and, with a howl of devilish despair and revenge, withdrew.

I left the room, and, locking the door, made a solemn vow in my own heart never to resume my labours; and then, with trembling steps, I sought my own bedroom. I was alone; none were near me to lift the gloom, and relieve me from the sickening terror of my thoughts.

I heard the sound of footsteps along outside the hut; the door opened, and the wretch whom I dreaded soon appeared. Shutting the door, he approached me, and said, in a smothered voice – "You have destroyed the work which you began; what is it that you intend? Do you dare to break your promise? I have endured toil and misery: I left Switzerland with you; I crept along the shores of the Rhine, among its willow islands, and over the summits of its hills. I have dwelt many months in the heaths of England, and among the deserts of Scotland. I have endured terrible tiredness, cold and hunger; do you dare destroy my hopes?"

"Begone! I do break my promise; never will I create another like yourself, equal in deformity and wickedness."

"As a slave I reasoned with you before, but you have proved yourself unworthy of my offer. Remember that I have power; you believe yourself miserable, but I can make you so wretched that the light of day will be hateful to you. You are my creator, but I am your master – obey!"

"The hour of my weakness is past, and the period of your power is arrived. Begone! I am firm, and your words will only enrage me."

"It is well. I go; but remember, I shall be with you on your wedding-night."

I started forward, and exclaimed:

"Villain! before you sign my death-warrant, be sure that you are yourself safe."

I would have seized him; but he eluded me, and quitted the house in a hurry: in a few moments I saw him in his boat, which shot across the waters with an arrowy swiftness, and was soon lost amidst the waves.

And then I thought again of his words; "I will be with you on your wedding-night."

That then was the period fixed for my doom. In that hour I should die, and at the same time satisfy and put out the flames of his malice. The thought did not move me to fear; yet when I thought of my beloved Elizabeth – of her tears and endless sorrow, when she should find her lover so cruelly snatched from her – tears, the first I had shed for many months, streamed from my eyes, and I decided not to fall before my enemy without a bitter struggle.

I would have been happy to live out my days alone on that island, but the very next day I saw a fishing-boat land close to me, and one of the men brought me a packet; it contained letters from Geneva, and one from Clerval, entreating me to join him. He said that nearly a year had elapsed since we had quitted Switzerland, and France was yet unvisited. He asked me, therefore, to leave my lonely island and meet him at Perth, in a week from that time, when we might arrange the plan of our future travels. This letter recalled me to life, and I decided to quit my island at the end of two days.

Yet, before I departed, there was a task to perform, on which I shuddered to reflect: I must pack my chemical instruments; and for that purpose, I must enter the room which had been the scene of my disgusting work, and I must handle those tools, the sight of which was sickening to me. The next morning, at daybreak, I summoned sufficient courage, and unlocked the door of my laboratory.

I gathered up my chemicals and the half-completed body and put them into a basket, with a great quantity of stones, and laying them up, determined to throw them into the sea that very night; and in the mean time I sat upon the beach, cleaning and arranging my chemical apparatus.

Between two and three in the morning the moon rose; and I then, putting my basket aboard a little skiff, sailed out about four miles from the shore. At one time the moon, which had before been clear, was suddenly overspread by a thick cloud, and I took advantage of the moment of darkness, and cast my basket into the sea; I listened to the gurgling sound as it sunk, and then sailed away from the spot. The sky became clouded; but the air was pure, although chilled by the north-east breeze that was then rising. But it refreshed me, and filled me with such agreeable feelings that I decided to extend my stay on the water, and fixing the rudder in a direct position, stretched myself at the bottom of the boat. Clouds hid the moon, everything was dark and hidden, and I heard only the sound of the boat as its keel cut through the waves; the murmur lulled me, and in a short time I slept soundly.

I do not know how long I remained like that, but when I awoke I found that the sun had already mounted considerably. The wind was high, and the waves continually threatened the safety of my little boat. I found that the wind was north-east, and must have driven me far from the coast from which I had embarked. I tried to change my course, but quickly found that if I again made the attempt the boat would be instantly filled with water from the crashing waves. Thus, my only option was to sail with the wind. I confess that I had a few feelings of terror. I had no compass with me, and was so little acquainted with the geography of this part of the world that the sun was of little benefit to me. I might be driven into the wide Atlantic, and feel all the tortures of starvation, or be swallowed up in the enormous waters that roared and battered my boat. I had already been out many hours, and felt the torment of a burning thirst, a prelude to my other sufferings. I looked on the heavens, which were covered by clouds that flew before the wind only to be replaced by others: I looked upon the sea, it was to be my grave.

"Fiend," I exclaimed, "your task is already fulfilled!"

I thought of Elizabeth, of my father, and of Clerval; and sank into a dream, so despairing and frightful, that even now, when the scene is on day in the bloom of health and hope, and the next a prey for worms and the decay of the tomb! Of what materials was I made, that I could thus resist so many shocks, which, like the turning of the wheel, continually renewed the torture?

Chapter Eighteen

However, death was not to release me so soon. In fact, further tortures awaited me when I spied land two days later. I washed up upon a beach in the dead of night. When I threw myself upon the sand, exhausted, I was immediately spied by two local men, who cried:

"Murderer! Seize him!"

In short, I found myself in an Irish dungeon, accused of murdering a man, found dead on the beach not far from my landing spot. It was only after almost a week that I discovered the dead man was Clerval!

How deep was my despair! How eagerly I sought death! But alas, all means of my own demise had been stripped from me; penknife, tie, bootlaces, even my belt!

I will not dwell on my sufferings, for my story is long, and there is still much to tell. After nearly three months, my father arrived to vouch for me, and the local magistrate became persuaded of my innocence.

I remember, as I quitted the prison, I heard one of the men say:

"He may be innocent of the murder, but he has certainly a bad conscience."

These words struck me. A bad conscience! Yes, surely I had one. William, Justine, and Clerval, had died through my cursed actions.

"And whose death," cried I, "is to finish the tragedy? Ah! my father, do not remain in this wretched country; take me where I may forget myself, my existence, and all the world."

In about a week later, we returned to Geneva. My cousin welcomed me with warm affection; yet tears were in her eyes, as she beheld my emaciated frame and feverish cheeks. I saw a change in her also. She was thinner, and had lost much of that heavenly life that had before charmed me; but her gentleness, and soft looks of compassion, made her a more fit companion for one blasted and miserable as I was.

Soon after my arrival my father spoke of my immediate marriage with my cousin. I remained silent.

"Have you, then, some other attachment?" he asked.

"None on earth. I love Elizabeth, and look forward to our wedding with delight. Let the day therefore be fixed; and on it I will dedicate myself, in life or death, to the happiness of my cousin."

"My dear Victor, do not speak thus. Heavy misfortunes have befallen us; but let us only cling closer to what remains, and transfer our love for those whom we have lost to those who yet live."

I remembered the words of the monster; and that when he had pronounced the words, "I shall be with you on your wedding-night," I should regard the threatened fate as unavoidable. But death was no evil to me, if the loss of Elizabeth occurred at the same time; and I therefore, with a contented and even cheerful countenance, agreed with my father, that if my cousin would consent, the ceremony should take place in ten days.

A house was purchased for us near Cologny, by which we should enjoy the pleasures of the country, and yet be so near Geneva as to see my father every day; who would still live within the walls, for the benefit of Ernest, that he might follow his studies at the schools.

I took every precaution to defend myself, in case the fiend should openly attack me. I carried pistols and a dagger constantly about me, and was ever on the watch to prevent any tricks and by these means gained a greater degree of peace.

On our Wedding Day, Elizabeth seemed happy; my happy face contributed greatly to calm her mind. But on the day that was to fulfil my wishes and my destiny, she was sad, and a fear of evil pervaded her; and perhaps also she thought of the dreadful secret, which I had promised to reveal to her the following day. My father was in the meantime overjoyed, and, in the bustle of preparation, only observed in the sadness of his niece the shyness of a bride.

After the ceremony was performed, a large party assembled at my father's; but it was agreed that Elizabeth and I should pass the afternoon and night at Evian, and return to Cologny the next morning. As the day was fair, and the wind favourable, we resolved to go by water.

Those were the last moments of my life during which I enjoyed the feeling of happiness. We passed rapidly along: the sun was hot, but we were sheltered from its rays by a kind of canopy, while we enjoyed the beauty of the scene, sometimes on one side of the lake, where we saw Mont Salêve, the pleasant banks of Montalêgre, and at a distance, above all, the beautiful Mont Blânc.

Chapter Nineteen

It was eight o'clock when we reached the house at Evian.

"Night is dreadful, very dreadful," I thought.

I passed an hour in this state of mind, when suddenly I reflected how dreadful the combat which I expected would be to my wife, and I asked her to go to bed, deciding not to join her until I had obtained some knowledge as to the situation of my enemy. She left me, and I continued some time walking up and down the passages of the house, and inspecting every corner that might provide a hiding place to my adversary. But I discovered no trace of him, and was beginning to believe that some luck had prevented his attack; when suddenly I heard a shrill and dreadful scream. It came from the room into which Elizabeth slept. As I heard it, the whole truth rushed into my mind, my arms dropped, the motion of every muscle and fibre was suspended; I could feel the blood trickling in my veins, and tingling in the extremities of my limbs. This state lasted but for an instant; the scream was repeated, and I rushed into the room.

Great God! why did I not then expire! Why am I here to relate the destruction of the best hope, and the purest creature of Earth. She was there, lifeless and inanimate, thrown across the bed, her head hanging down, and her pale and distorted features half covered by her hair. Everywhere I turn I see the same figure – her bloodless arms and relaxed form flung by the murderer on its bridal bier. Could I behold this, and live? Alas! life is obstinate, and clings closest where it is most hated. For a moment only did I lose recollection; I fainted. When I recovered, I found myself surrounded by the people of the inn; their countenances expressed a breathless terror. The murderous mark of the fiend's grasp was on her neck, and the breath had ceased to issue from her lips.

While I still hung over her in the agony of despair, I happened to look up. The windows of the room had before been darkened; and I felt a kind of panic on seeing the pale, yellow light of the moon illuminate the chamber. The shutters had been thrown back; and, with a feeling of horror I saw at the open window a figure most hideous. A grin was on the face of the monster; he seemed to jeer, as with his fiendish finger he pointed towards the corpse of my wife. I rushed towards the window, and drawing a pistol from my bosom, shot; but he eluded me, leaped from his position, and, running with the swiftness of lightning, plunged into the lake.

The report of the pistol brought the crowd to my side. I pointed to the spot where he had disappeared, and we followed the track with boats; nets were cast, but in vain. After passing several hours, we returned hopeless, most of my companions believing it to have been a form that I had imagined. After having landed, they proceeded to search the country, parties going in different directions among the woods and vines.

I did not go with them. The death of William, the execution of Justine, the murder of Clerval, and lastly of my wife; even at that moment I knew not that my only remaining friends were safe from the evil of the fiend; my father even now might be writhing under his grasp, and Ernest might be dead at his feet. This idea made me shudder, and returned me to action. I jumped up, and decided to return to Geneva with all possible speed. There were no horses to be found, and I had to return by the lake; but the wind was against me, and the rain fell in torrents. However, it was hardly morning, and I might reasonably hope to arrive by night. I hired men to row, and took an oar myself, for I had always experienced relief from mental torment in bodily exercise. But the overflowing misery I now felt, and the excess of agitation that I endured, rendered me incapable of any exertion. I threw down the oar;

and, leaning my head upon my hands, gave way to every gloomy idea that arose.

I arrived at Geneva. My father and Ernest yet lived; but the former sunk under the tidings that I bore. I see him now, excellent and respected old man! bore. His eyes wandered, empty, for they had lost their charm and their delight – his niece, his more than daughter, whom he cared for with all that affection which a man feels, who, at the end of life, having few affections, clings more tightly to those that remain. Cursed, cursed be the fiend that brought misery on his grey hairs, and doomed him to waste in wretchedness! He could not live under the horrors that were accumulated around him; a fit was brought on, and in a few days, he died in my arms.

All this destruction wrought by the monster! I was possessed by a maddening rage when I thought of him, and desired and prayed that I might have him within my grasp to wreak a great and final revenge on his cursed head.

Chapter Twenty

My first action was to quit Geneva for ever; my country, which, when I was happy and beloved, was dear to me, now, in my troubles, became hateful. I gathered a sum of money, together with a few jewels which had belonged to my mother, and departed. And now my wanderings began, which are to cease only with my death. I have crossed a vast portion of the earth, and have endured all the hardships which travellers, in deserts and distant countries, always meet. How I have lived I hardly know; many times, have I stretched my failing limbs upon the sandy plain, and prayed for death. But revenge kept me alive; I dared not die and leave my enemy alive.

"By the sacred earth on which I kneel!" I cried, "by the shades that wander near me, by the deep and eternal grief that I feel; I swear; and by thee, O Night, and by the spirits that watch over you, I swear to pursue the demon, who caused this misery, until he or I shall perish in conflict."

I was answered through the stillness of night by a loud and fiendish laugh. It rung on my ears long and heavily; the mountains re-echoed it, and I felt as if all hell surrounded me with mockery and laughter. Surely in that moment I should have been possessed by frenzy, and have destroyed my miserable existence, but that my vow was heard, and that I was reserved for revenge. The laughter died away; when a well-known and disgusting voice, apparently close to my ear, addressed me in a whisper – "I am satisfied: miserable wretch, you have decided to live, and I am satisfied."

I darted towards the spot from which the sound came; but the devil eluded my grasp. Suddenly the broad disk of the moon arose, and shone full upon his ghastly and distorted shape, as he fled with more than mortal speed.

I pursued him; and for many months this has been my task. I followed the fiend to Russia, where he turned north. As I still pursued my journey to the northward, the snows thickened, and the cold increased in a degree almost too severe to survive. The peasants were shut up in their huts, and only a few of the most hardy ventured forth to seize the animals whom starvation had forced from their hiding-places to seek for prey. The rivers were covered with ice, and no fish could be caught; and thus I was cut off from my chief source of food.

I resolved not to fail in my purpose; and, calling on heaven to support me, I continued to cross immense deserts, until the ocean appeared at a distance, and formed the horizon. Oh! how unlike it was to the blue seas of the south! Covered with ice, it was only to be distinguished from land by its superior wildness and ruggedness.

Some weeks before this period I had procured a sledge and dogs, and thus crossed the snows with incredible speed. I know not whether the fiend possessed the same advantages; but I found that, as before I had daily lost ground in the pursuit, I now gained on him; so much so, that when I first saw the ocean, he was but one day's journey in advance, and I hoped to intercept him before he should reach the beach.

I exchanged my land sledge for one made for the frozen ocean; and, purchasing a plentiful stock of provisions, I departed from land.

I cannot guess how many days have passed since then; but I have endured misery, which nothing but the eternal desire for revenge burning in my heart.

But now, when I appeared almost within grasp of my enemy, my hopes were suddenly blown out, and I lost all trace of him more completely than I had ever done before. A crashing of ice was heard; the thunder of its progress, as the waters rolled and swelled beneath me, became every moment more terrific. I pressed on, but in vain. The wind arose; the sea roared; and, as with the mighty shock of an earthquake, it split, and cracked with a tremendous and overwhelming sound. The work was soon finished: in a few minutes a rough sea rolled between me and my enemy, and I was left drifting on a scattered piece of ice, that was continually shrinking, and thus preparing for me a hideous death.

In this manner many appalling hours passed; several of my dogs died; and I myself was about to sink under distress, when I saw your vessel riding at anchor, giving me hopes of life. I had no idea that vessels ever came so far north, and was amazed at the sight. I quickly destroyed part of my sledge to construct oars; and by these means was enabled, with infinite fatigue, to move my ice-raft in the direction of your ship.

Oh! when will my guiding spirit, in leading me to the demon, allow me the rest I so much desire; or must I die, and he yet live? If I do, swear to me, Walton, that he shall not escape; that you will seek him, and satisfy my revenge with his death. Yet, do I dare ask you to undertake my task, to endure the hardships that I have undergone? No; I am not so selfish. Yet, when I am dead, if he should appear; if fortune should bring him to you, swear that he shall not live – swear that he shall not triumph over all my woes, and live to make another such a wretch as I am. He is persuasive; and once his words had even power over my heart; but trust him not. His soul is as hellish as his form, full of treachery and fiend-like evil. Don't listen to him; call on the spirits of William, Justine, Clerval, Elizabeth, my father, and of the wretched Victor, and thrust your sword into his heart. I will hover near, and direct the steel to its target.

Turquoise Ice in Northern Russia

Chapter Twenty-One

Captain Walton. August 26th

You have read this strange and terrific story, and do you not feel your blood thickened with horror, like that which even now thickens mine? Sometimes, seized with sudden agony, Frankenstein could not continue his tale; at others, his voice broken, yet piercing, uttered with difficulty the words so full of agony.

Frankenstein discovered that I made notes concerning his history: he asked to see them, and then himself corrected and added to them in many places; but mainly in giving the life and spirit to the conversations he held with his enemy.

"Since you have preserved my story," said he, "I wouldn't want a mutilated one to go down in history."

Captain Walton. September 2nd.

I am surrounded by mountains of ice, which gives of no escape, and threaten every moment to crush my vessel. The brave fellows, whom I have persuaded to be my companions, look towards me for aid; but I have none to give. There is something terribly appalling in our situation, yet my courage and hopes do not desert me. We may survive; and if we do not, I will repeat the lessons of the Roman, Seneca, and die with a good heart.

Captain Walton. September 19th.

Frankenstein has died.

Great God! what a scene has just taken place! I am still dizzy with the memory of it. I hardly know whether I shall have the power to tell it; yet the tale which I have recorded would be incomplete without this final and wonderful catastrophe. I entered the cabin, where lay the remains of my ill-fated and admirable friend. Over him hung a form which I cannot find words to describe; gigantic in height, yet foul and distorted in its shape. As he hung over the coffin, his face was concealed by long locks of ragged hair; but one vast hand was extended, in colour and apparent texture like that of a mummy. When he heard the sound of my approach, he ceased to utter words of grief and horror, and sprung towards the window. Never did I see a vision so horrible as his face, of such horrible, appalling ugliness. I shut my eyes and tried to recall what were my duties with regard to this destroyer. I called on him to stay.

"This is also my victim!" he cried. "In his murder my crimes are finally completed; the miserable story of my life is wound to its close! Oh, Frankenstein! generous and self-devoted being! Alas, he is cold; he cannot answer me!"

He sprang from the cabin-window, as he said this, upon the ice-raft which lay close to the vessel. He was soon borne away by the waves, and lost in darkness and distance.

The End

Ship Caught in Pack Ice

Biography of Lazlo Ferran

Educated near Oxford, during English author Lazlo Ferran's extraordinary life, he has been an aeronautical engineering student, dispatch rider, graphic designer, full-time busker, guitarist and singer, recording two albums. Having grown up in rural Buckinghamshire Lazlo says:

"The beautiful Chiltern Hills offered the ideal playground for a child's mind, in contrast to the ultra-strict education system of Bucks."

After a long and successful career within the science industry, Lazlo Ferran left to concentrate on writing.

Printed in Great Britain
by Amazon

76774268R00037